Delicious!

Helen Cooper

Picture Corgi

Deep in the woods it was lunchtime,
munchtime,
should have been cooking time,
down at the old white cabin.

But out in the garden there was rustling,
and scuffling,
a bit of a kerfuffling.
The sound of a Duck
and a Squirrel
and a Cat,
looking for a pumpkin in the pumpkin patch.

They hadn't found a single ripe one.

Pumpkin Soup,
all they ever wanted,
all they ever cooked in the old white cabin.
"We might have to make something different today,"
they agreed.

Back at the cabin, the Cat drew down
a faded old book.
  They blew off the cobwebs
  and, turning the pages,
    they wondered what else they could cook?

"Fish Soup!" said the Cat. "That sounds **scrumptious!**"
"Nutritious!" said the Squirrel.
"Delicious?" said the Duck.

So they all went fishing,
and that afternoon
the Duck caught four little tiddlers.

The Squirrel caught only a cold.

But the Cat caught twenty-two
beautiful trout, and they
brought them back to
the old white cabin.

INGREDIENTS

CHOP

STIR

WEIGH

The Cat sliced the fish
and popped them in the pot.
The Squirrel stirred,
while the Duck scooped up a pipkin of salt
with a pinch of pepper,
and tipped them in.

"It's scrumptious!" said the Cat.
"Nutritious!" said the Squirrel.

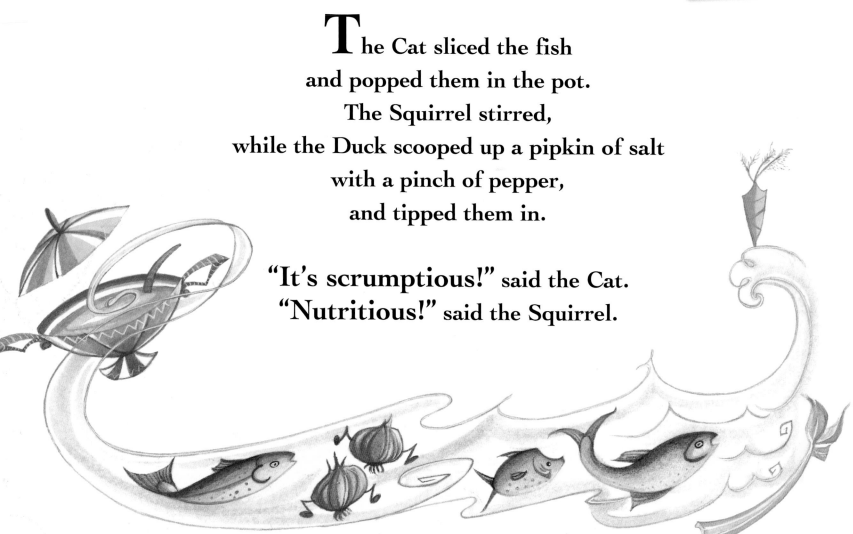

SEASON AND
SIMMER

But the Duck sniffed the soup and said,

"YUK!"

He wouldn't even try it.

Fish Soup.

   The best you ever tasted?

      Most of the soup was going to be wasted.

         They turned the pages of their recipe book

           and wondered what else they could cook.

"Mushroom Soup," said the Squirrel.

    "That sounds **scrumptious!**"

So they all went mushrooming.

Soon the Duck found a toadstool.

The Cat found something worse.

But the Squirrel found a mound of mushrooms.
And they carried them back to the old white cabin.

Mushroom Soup.
Would it be wasted?
Time for the Mushroom Soup to be tasted.

"Scrumptious!" squeaked the Squirrel.
"Nutritious?" said the Cat.
But the Duck sniffed the soup and said,

"YUK!"

He wouldn't even try it.

He went to bed feeling hungry,
with horrid pains in his tummy,
and dreamt of Spider Soup.

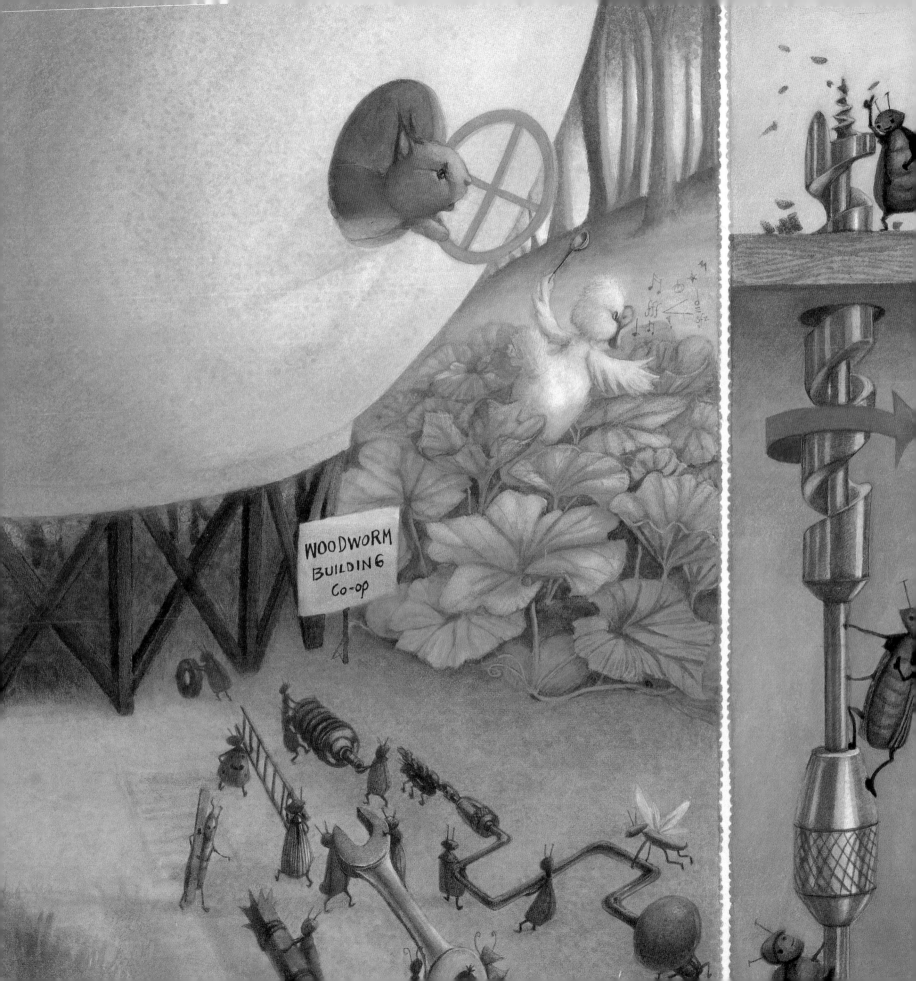

WOODWORM
BUILDING
Co-op

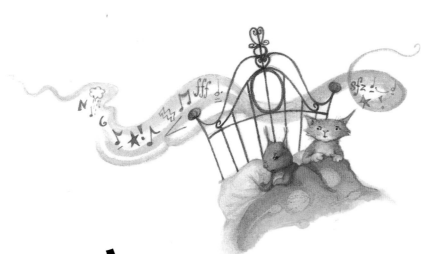

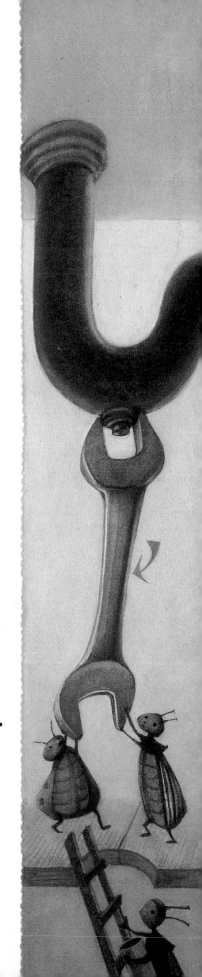

At peep of dawn, there was no peace
for the Cat and Squirrel,
trying to sleep in the old white cabin.
The Duck was hunting for a pumpkin,
hoping one had ripened.
"All I want is Pumpkin Soup," he mumbled,
and his hungry tummy rumbled
and he began to cry.

The Cat remembered it was market day.
"Perhaps we could buy a pumpkin," he said.

"Let's go!" quacked the Duck, and he ran off ahead with the basket.

GOOD
for
SOUP

At the woodland market there were vegetable stalls,
heaped tall
with peas
and beans
and aubergines
and onions
and parsnips.
Sadly, not a pumpkin to be seen.

And soon the Duck grumbled that his feet were sore,
and he cried, and he fussed, and whined to go home.

"Buy something quick!" said the Cat.
So the Squirrel bought some beetroot.

"That's brown and ugly!"
bawled the Duck.
But the Cat and the Squirrel were keen to leave.

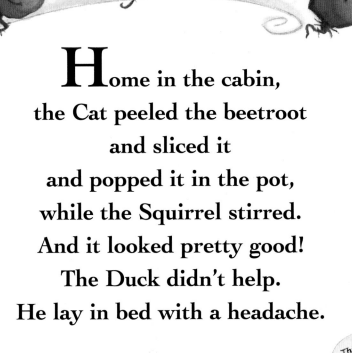

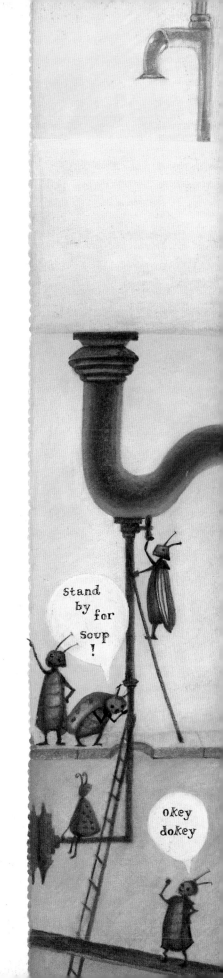

Home in the cabin,
the Cat peeled the beetroot
and sliced it
and popped it in the pot,
while the Squirrel stirred.
And it looked pretty good!
The Duck didn't help.
He lay in bed with a headache.

That's what happens when you don't eat.

Beetroot Soup.
The best you ever tasted.
Made by the Cat and the Squirrel
for the Duck,
who took one look and said . . .

stand by for soup!

okey dokey

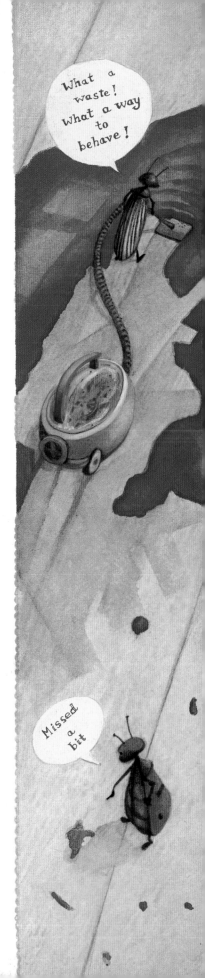

"I'm not eating that. **It's pink!**"

"You deserve to starve!"
growled the Squirrel.
"But all I want is Pumpkin Soup,"
howled the Duck.
"And that's orange!"

Then there was trouble.
A horrible squabble,
a hullabaloo in the old white cabin.

"**I**'ll trick him," whispered the Cat.

While the others ran a bath,
he slipped away with the basket again.
This time he bought some yellow courgettes,
the ripest tomatoes
and carrots,
and corn.

When no one was watching, he peeled them

and sliced them

and chopped them

and diced them

and squished them

and plopped them

into the cooking pot.

"That ought to do," he said to himself.
"Exactly the colour of Pumpkin Soup."

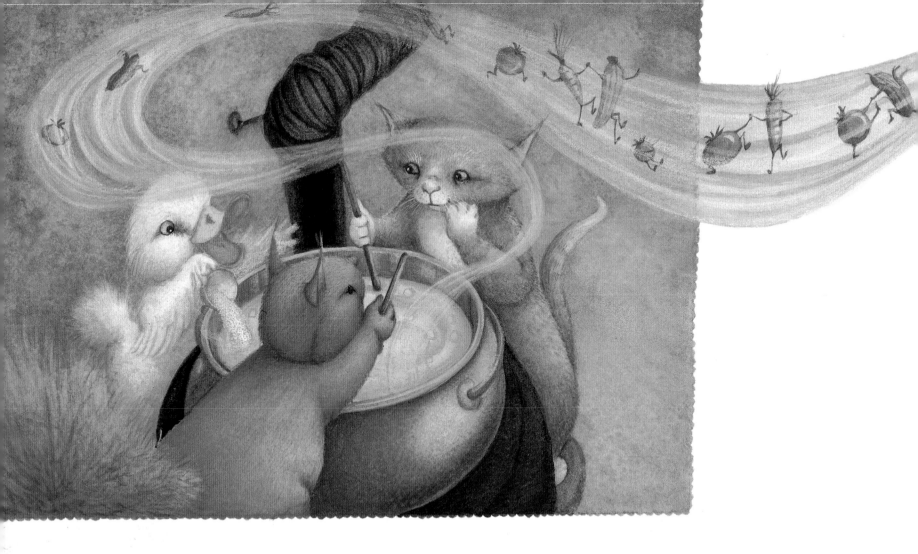

$\mathbf{T}$he Duck peered into the cooking pot.
"That looks like Pumpkin Soup!" he said.
He rushed to scoop up a pipkin of salt with a pinch of pepper
and tipped them in, while the Squirrel stirred.

They all stirred,

and soon it was soup-slurping time.

"Scrumptious?" said the Cat.

"Nutritious?" said the Squirrel.

The hungry Duck had another look.
He sniffed the soup suspiciously
and quacked,
"This isn't Pumpkin Soup . . ."